MW00892058

Marvin's Christmas

Jeanette C. Allen

Copyright © 2023 Jeanette C. Allen
All rights reserved
First Edition

Fulton Books
Meadville, PA

Published by Fulton Books 2023

ISBN 979-8-88982-439-8 (paperback)
ISBN 979-8-88982-440-4 (digital)

Printed in the United States of America

This book is dedicated to anyone who enjoys reading poems—sometimes zany and funny and always with love! With extra hugs to my children and grandchildren, who listened when I read each one to them.

Sleepy Marvin woke up from his nap.

His stomach was growling. He needed a snack.

He scurried to peek out of his hole. Down
the hall to the kitchen was his goal.

Someone had baked cookies, he squealed with delight.
He took some cheese and one cookie to save for tonight.

On the way back, he had to stop.
To admire the tree with a star on top.

Tonight comes the man to leave gifts underneath,
but only if you've been good is the belief.

Ah, Christmas is joyful thought Marvin the mouse, as he continued his way down the hall of the house.

All of a sudden, he saw the cat!
That looked like it was ready to attack!
His heartbeat grew rapid, his fur stood on end!

When the cat caught up and purred,
"Merry Christmas, Marvin!"

Ah, the Christmas spirit was in the cat, and Marvin was very thankful for that!

'Tis the time of goodwill and cheer, for
Marvin survives another year.

Merry Christmas and Happy New Year!
From Marvin the Mouse and all the gang here.

The End.

About the Author

Jeanette C. Allen

USPS carrier—soon to retire.

Married with three children, all grown up, and eight grandchildren.

Lives in Arcade, New York, with her husband, Lee.

Printed in the USA
CPSIA information can be obtained
at www.ICGtesting.com
LVHW061530251023
762115LV00008B/222